ZOE
to the
RESCUE

BELLA'S BROKEN LEG

Sherry B. Sauskojus
&
Vicki V. Lucas

Bella's Broken Leg

Fiction on Fire
ZoeRescues@gmail.com
www.ZoetotheRescue.com

Ordering Information:
Quantity sales. Special discounts are available on quantity purchases by corporations, associations, and others. For details, contact the publisher at the address above.

Book and cover design by Jansina of Rivershore Books.
Illustrations by Alyssa Mehlhorn.
The text is set in "Kelmscott Roman NF."
The display type is "Devious."

ISBN-10: 1975610989
ISBN-13: 978-1975610982

Printed in the United States of America
10   9   8   7   6   5   4   3   2   1

Dedication

To those who paved the way for us – both our parents and the first EMTs.

Zoe ran past the police cars.

She didn't even look at the fire trucks!

She was going straight to . . .

THE AMBULANCE!

She loved the lights
and the siren.

But inside was better!

The ambulance had many
things to help people, like . . .

stretchers,

stethoscopes,

and

bandages.

Josh and Nicole were preparing the equipment for the day.

"Can I go today?" Zoe asked.

"Do you remember the rules?" Josh asked.

"I sure do!" Zoe said.

Rule Number 1
Walk. Don't Run!

Rule Number 2
911 Helps You!

Rule Number 3
Look and See!

Josh's radio buzzed.

"911 Headquarters!
A six-year-old girl fell out of a
tree at Sunset Park.
Possible broken leg!"

Zoe dashed to get her pack.
She had bandages, a blanket,
and a stethoscope.

What did she need to help a
broken leg?

She couldn't ask.
It was time to go now!

Zoe jumped in the front seat.
Nicole was driving.
"Seat belt!" Nicole said.

The buckle snapped into place.
The station doors flew open.
The ambulance roared out.
The siren filled the air!

A boy was waiting for them at the park.

"She's by the big tree," he said.
"But my mom is waiting. I
have to go."

"Good job for calling 911,"
Nicole said.

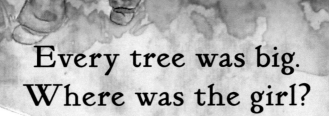

Every tree was big.
Where was the girl?

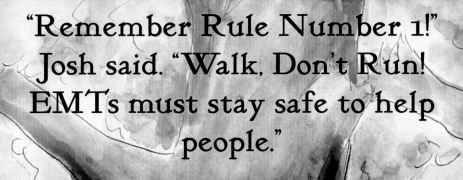

"Remember Rule Number 1!"
Josh said. "Walk, Don't Run!
EMTs must stay safe to help
people."

Zoe searched but didn't see
anyone.

And then . . .

Something pink was
under a large branch.
A girl lay trapped on
the ground.

"Help!" she called.

Zoe ran to the girl. There was
a loud crack, and Zoe jumped
back. A branch landed right in
front of her!

She forgot to stay safe.

**Rule Number One -
Walk, Don't Run!**

"Please help me!" the girl cried.

Zoe looked at the trees. Safe!

Zoe walked this time, but she had to decide fast. She had bandages, a blanket, and a stethoscope.

What could she do to help?

Zoe remembered the
second rule.

**Rule Number Two -
911 Helps You!**

This meant to call for help.
Zoe called out as loud as she
could. "She's here! Come help!"

"We'll be right there!"
Nicole yelled.

Now what could she do?
Then she remembered!

**Rule Number Three -
Look and See!**

The girl wasn't bleeding.
No bandages.

The stethoscope
was for heart
and lungs.
Not legs.

Zoe looked
again. The
girl shook and
shivered.

She was cold!

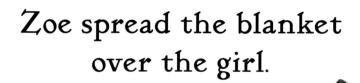

Zoe spread the blanket
over the girl.

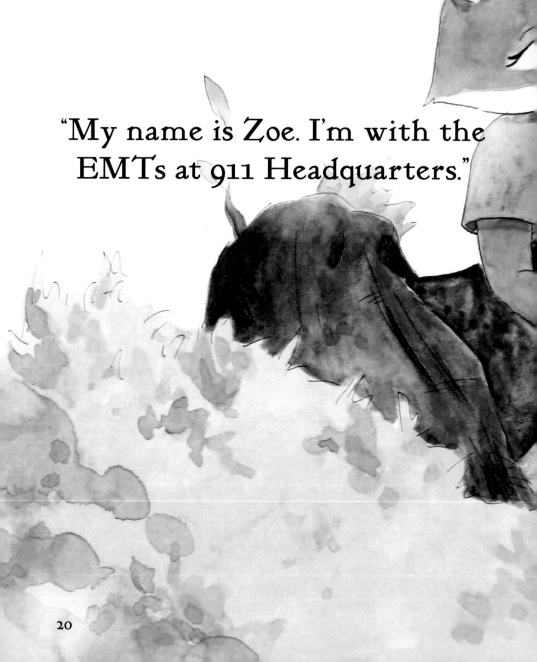

"My name is Zoe. I'm with the
EMTs at 911 Headquarters."

"I'm Bella," she said. "My leg hurts."

The EMTs came with
bags of supplies.

Josh carried a
small backboard.

Josh knelt beside Bella.
"How do you feel?" he asked.

"Not very good." Bella sniffed.

Nicole lifted the branch
off Bella.

Josh got special scissors.
"I'm going to cut your pants to
look at your leg and feel if it's
broken."

"Ow!" Bella cried.

"Sorry," Josh said. "It's going to
hurt a bit, but I have to do it
to get you to the hospital."

"This is a neck brace so your neck doesn't move," Nicole said.

Then Zoe helped Nicole put splints around the leg to keep it still when they carried her to the ambulance.

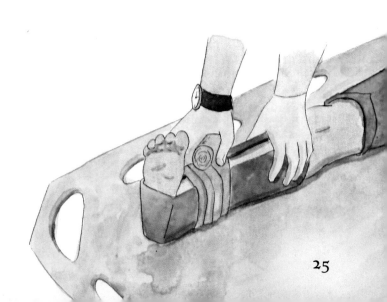

They put Bella on the board
and put straps like seatbelts
over her.

"The board will keep you extra
safe while we go to the
hospital," said Nicole.

"Then the doctor will take pictures of your bones to see if any are broken."

They placed a head roll
around her head.

"To make you comfortable,"
Nicole said.

Josh and Nicole lifted the board and carried Bella to the ambulance.

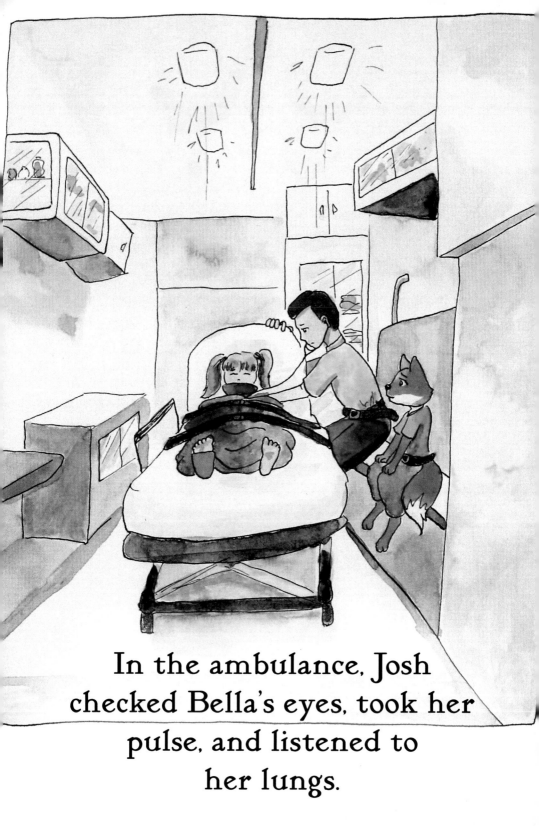

In the ambulance, Josh
checked Bella's eyes, took her
pulse, and listened to
her lungs.

Bella's mom was waiting
at the hospital.

Nicole pushed the stretcher
into the hospital. When
Nicole came back, they
cleaned the ambulance, put up
the equipment, and drove to
911 Headquarters.

The radio beeped again. "911 Headquarters. Bella has one broken leg, but she will be okay!"

They cheered.

"Great work today," Josh said. "You remembered your three rules and helped Bella.

"We want to make you a junior EMT."

"So I can come tomorrow and help more people?" Zoe asked.

"You bet!" Josh said.

"Yay!" Zoe shouted.

She couldn't wait to learn more about the ambulance and to rescue anyone who needs help.

She was ready for the next siren . . .

Did You Know . . .

EMT stands for Emergency Medical Technician. People who work on an ambulance study for a long time to learn how to help people.

The blue star on the ambulance is called a Star of Life. All around the world, this star shows that emergency medical people are here to help.

Bones are inside your body, making you strong. Adults have 207 bones!

The biggest bone is in your leg. It's called the femur.

Bones are very strong. It takes a hard fall to break them.

Calcium is good for your bones. Drink lots of milk and eat cheese to make your bones stronger.

An x-ray is a camera that can take pictures of your bones! Then a doctor can see if the bones are broken.

After the doctor sees you have a broken bone, she will put a cast on it to make sure it grows back straight.

Stock Your Own First Aid Kit

Zoe had her pack of supplies ready to go so that when an emergency happened, she had everything she might need.

Want to have your own?

Here's how.

1. **Find a bag large enough for your supplies.**

   This could be a backpack like Zoe has or perhaps a special bag you buy at the store that has the Star of Life on it.

2. **Fill it with important supplies.**

   Here's a list to get you started.
   - Alcohol pads
   - Antiseptic wipes
   - Band-aids of all sizes
   - Elastic bandages
   - Hand sanitizer
   - Disposable gloves
   - Cotton balls and Q-tips
   - A blanket, if it fits

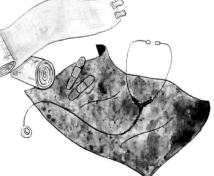

 Sherry B. Sauskojus always responded to someone's injury with "Oh, cool. Can I help?" She began work as an EMT at age 17 and has never lost the love for the work. Together with Mr. Booboo Bear, she has led countless tours with thousands of children due to her belief in the importance of educating the community about EMS.

Vicki V. Lucas didn't find the urge to continue in the emergency medical field after her first responder's course. Instead she turned to fiction writing where she writes fantasy and  supernatural thrillers. Find out more at www.vickivlucas.com

Made in United States
North Haven, CT
26 October 2023

43204120R00024